MW00909590

THE ADVENTURES OF

lucyloo & Roo ™

...AND THE MAGIC OF THE GRATITUDE STICK!

DR. STACEY SCOTT & KYRA SCOTT

ORIGINAL CHARACTER DESIGN BY DANIKA SCOTT
ARTWORK BY PIA REYES

OUR MISSION STATEMENT

Helping our children find inspiration and empowerment through personal experience and imagination, to draw strength from adversity, and to step forward in confidence... all by learning to

"JUST GRATITUDE IT!"

For us this isn't just a story. It is a movement. Our purpose is to share and educate as many people, groups, and charities as possible. Visit our website for more details.

www.lucylooandroo.com

Lucy wakes up. Her hair is a tangled mess.

"MOM!",

she yells in total distress.

"MOM LOOK AT MY HAIR! I CAN'T DO ANYTHING WITH IT!"

Her brother, Matt and her sister, Pippa chime in...

"LOOK IT'S LUCY-LOO, LUCY-LOO, LUCY-LOO WITH THE WEIRD HAIRDO!"

Lucy's mom scolds them saying, "Stop that you two! Relax Loo. We are going to the hairdresser today. She will fix it for you."

"Mom you were right!
She did fix it! I love my new hairdo!
THANK YOU!
THANK YOU!
THANK YOU!"

Lucy and her Mom arrive back home just as
her best friend Tallulah is being dropped off.
Lucy jumps out of the car full of excitement!

"TALLULAH DO
YOU LIKE MY NEW HAIR?"

Tallulah squeals with glee,

"I LOVE YOUR
HAIRDO LOO!"

Lucy beams with happiness as she feels she now
looks just like Tallulah and her big sister Pippa.

Lucy and Tallulah play in the sprinkler, chase
Roo and search for Fairies. When suddenly...

"LUCY! LOOK!
IT'S A FAIRY! AND IT'S ON
THAT DRAGONFLY!"

"WHAT? REALLY??"
Lucy is as excited as Tallulah,
"Let's follow it!"

The girls and Roo chase after the dragonfly
when Lucy yells,

"WAIT I'M STUCK!"

Tallulah turns around to see Lucy's hair
caught in a tree, "Oh no Lucy your
curls are caught on that branch!"

Lucy, with a puzzled look on her

face says, "WHAT? WHAT
CURLS? MY HAIR IS
STRAIGHT LIKE YOURS!"

What Lucy doesn't realize is that the water
from the sprinkler has made her curls return.

Tallulah reaches up to help free Lucy.

"OUCH!"

Lucy cries. Tallulah softly says, "Sorry Loo."

As the branch breaks Lucy falls back into the bushes, hurting herself even more.

"OUCH ROO!
THAT HURTS!"

Lucy's eyes begin to fill with
tears as she tries to get up.

She runs back to the house
crying, as Tallulah and
Roo chase after her.

Lucy runs past her
Mom and slams her
bedroom door.

"TALLULAH
WHAT HAPPENED?"

"I don't know. Her hair got caught in the branches. I tried to help but she fell."

"I'll go check on Loo," says Lucy's Mom, "There is some food in the kitchen for you and Roo."

"Lucy are you okay?"
Lucy cries,
"MY HAIR IS CURLY AGAIN!
I THOUGHT THE HAIRDRESSER
MADE IT STRAIGHT!"

"OH NO LOO, Your hair was
straight today because that's how the hairdresser
styled it... Lucy, your curls are so beautiful, don't
you like them?" Lucy answers with a frown,
"NO! I hate them! The kids at school
make fun of me, they say Lucy-Loo with
her curly doo belongs in the zoo!"

"Lucy I'm sorry they say hurtful things, You are so very special."
Muffled, Lucy responds, "HUH! THEN WHY DO THEY
TEASE ME?" "Lucy you have to realize kids who tease others
are usually not very happy inside. Some even choose to hurt others
because they think it will make them feel better about themselves."

"REALLY?"

asks Lucy. "Yes, when others tease you or call you names, they are usually hurt themselves,

WE NEED TO HAVE COMPASSION AND BE KIND TO THEM."

"I GET IT LUCY. When I do my hair, or put on a nice dress, I would like other people to like how I look, but they have the right not to. However, when they tell you that or tease you about something, then we have to have compassion and understand that something may not be right in their heart or in their life."

"BUT WHY PICK ME TO TEASE?" asks Lucy. "That's the thing Lucy, it isn't about you, we must love ourselves and be grateful for who we are. When we do that, no one can hurt us no matter what they say."

"The work starts INSIDE YOUR HEAD AND YOUR HEART, we need to be thankful for who we are and own our own uniqueness. That makes us special and that's what makes you special."

"THE WORK STARTS WITH GRATEFUL
THOUGHTS INSIDE YOUR HEAD
AND LINGERS WITH GRATEFUL
FEELINGS INSIDE YOUR HEART."

Lucy jumps up and hugs her Mom, "THANKS MOM YOU ALWAYS MAKE ME FEEL BETTER."

"Come on Lucy, let's go downstairs. Tallulah and Roo are waiting for you."

Lucy feels so much better after talking with her mom, so she joins Tallulah and Roo and happily eats as Tallulah excitedly chats about going back outside to search for more Fairies.

The girls and Roo spend the rest of the
evening playing in the yard, running through the
sprinkler and of course searching for those Fairies.

As the night approaches the girls get ready to camp in Lucy's backyard.

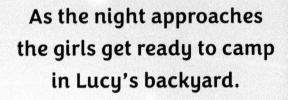

"ROO, YOU NEED TO LET THIS GO, WE NEED TO GO TO SLEEP."

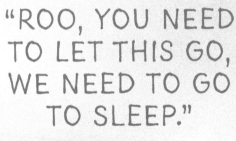

Roo could sense there was something special about the stick.

Lucy, Tallulah and Roo
fall fast asleep.

As the girls sleep
peacefully, Lucy's Mom
and Dad watch over them.

Suddenly, the tent begins to sparkle!
Roo bolts up. Hovering above him are what
appear to be

FAIRIES!

Lucy sleepily wakes up,
"WHO'S THERE?"

The Fairies in unison say,
"DON'T BE AFRAID LUCY, WE ARE THE MAGICAL FOREST FAIRIES. WE HAVE COME TO TELL YOU ABOUT THE MAGIC OF THE GRATITUDE STICK!"

"wHAT?"
questions Lucy,
"A Gratitude Stick? This is
just a broken branch that
got caught in my hair!"

"NO LUCY," chime the Fairies,
"IT IS PART OF OUR MAGICAL
FAIRY TREE AND IT CHOSE YOU!"

"Really?
What does it do?"

The Fairies answer, "LUCY, WHEN YOU HOLD IT TIGHT WITHIN YOUR HANDS IT HELPS YOU TO SEE ALL THE WONDERFUL THINGS IN YOUR LIFE AND ALL THE THINGS YOU SHOULD BE GRATEFUL FOR! CLOSE YOUR EYES AND FEEL IT!"

Lucy closes her eyes and the stick begins to glow and change.

"YES, YES,
I FEEL SOMETHING,
SOMETHING WONDERFUL!"

The Fairies respond,
"WHAT YOU ARE FEELING LUCY IS THE POWER
OF GRATITUDE!
**Now go back to sleep and dream
grateful thoughts."**

**The Fairies then sprinkle pixie dust on
the girls and Roo, and softly sing:**

"WE ARE GIFTING YOU AN ATTITUDE OF GRATITUDE.
IT'S A FEELING, AND IT'S HEALING,
IT'S A WAY OF BEING AND SEEING,
FOR YOU CHANGE YOUR DAY, BY WHAT YOU SAY!
BE GRATEFUL AND NEVER HATEFUL,
IF TEASED, TAKE IT WITH EASE.
LOVE EVERYONE, AND ALWAYS HAVE FUN!
HOLD PEACE IN YOUR HEART, FOR YOU'RE BOTH
SO SMART!
DREAM BIG GOALS, YOU SPECIAL SOULS!
AND IT IS WITH THIS WISH, THAT WE GIVE THIS
GIFT! SO USE YOUR WIT AND JUST GRATITUDE IT!"

Tallulah wakes up to Roo's bum in her face and says "Roo, what are you doing? What is in your mouth?"

Lucy and Tallulah both hold their Gratitude sticks and Lucy exclaims, "Tallulah, the Fairies were here last night and they gave each of us magical

GRATITUDE STICKS!"

Tallulah surprised by the sticks says,
"GRATITUDE STICKS,
FAIRIES .... NO WAY!"

"YES, they were here and they are
real! The branch that got caught in my
hair was from their magical tree!"

As both girls hold their sticks Tallulah asks,
"HOW DOES IT WORK?"

"IT IS SO EASY,
keep holding it and think of something you
are grateful for and say it out loud!"

Tallulah closes her eyes and begins
to feel so happy inside and then shouts,

"OH LUCY,
I'M SO GRATEFUL YOU ARE
MY VERY BEST FRIEND!"

The girls excitedly tell their parents about their
MAGICAL NIGHT, THE FAIRIES,
THE GRATITUDE STICKS
AND HOW THEY WORK!

Tallulah's Dad holds one of the Gratitude Sticks and says "Amazing, you girls have been blessed with the gift of Gratitude. Mother Earth looks after all of us. We have everything we need, we only have to see that and be grateful for what we have and who we are. When we can do that and feel that, then everything changes! That is the power of Gratitude!"

Tallulah and Lucy HUG each other good-bye,
feeling the immense warmth and love of Gratitude.

That evening Lucy shares her story of the Fairies, her curly hair and how she learned to "Just Gratitude It!" Her brother and sister both listen in awe and they too feel the power and love of Gratitude! Pippa takes the Gratitude Stick and says "I FEEL IT! IT'S LIKE A HEALTHY SELFIE STICK!" Matt exclaims "Cool name!" It was then, that the nightly tradition of saying what they were Grateful for began!

Lucy often sleeps with the Gratitude Stick, either in her hand or beside her bed. It is on these nights that Lucy dreams of all the things she is grateful for and is visited by the magical Forest Fairies. Lucy now loves her hair, her beautiful curls and has developed an
ATTITUDE of GRATITUDE
making everyday a blessing.

◆ FriesenPress

SUITE 300 - 990 FORT ST
VICTORIA, BC, V8V 3K2
CANADA

WWW.FRIESENPRESS.COM

COPYRIGHT © 2021 BY DR. STACEY SCOTT AND KYRA SCOTT
FIRST EDITION — 2021

ALL RIGHTS RESERVED.

NO PART OF THIS PUBLICATION MAY BE REPRODUCED
IN ANY FORM, OR BY ANY MEANS, ELECTRONIC OR
MECHANICAL, INCLUDING PHOTOCOPYING, RECORDING, OR
ANY INFORMATION BROWSING, STORAGE, OR RETRIEVAL
SYSTEM, WITHOUT PERMISSION IN WRITING FROM
FRIESENPRESS.

ISBN
978-1-5255-9037-5 (HARDCOVER)
978-1-5255-9036-8 (PAPERBACK)
978-1-5255-9038-2 (EBOOK)

1. JUVENILE FICTION, FANTASY & MAGIC

DISTRIBUTED TO THE TRADE BY THE
INGRAM BOOK COMPANY

ABOUT THE AUTHORS

Dr. Scott is a Chiropractic Sports Specialist and has built her own multi-disciplinary wellness clinic located on Vancouver Island. Her daughter, Kyra, has a background in counselling specializing in substance abuse and addiction. She is currently working as a mental health support worker and a business entrepreneur. They believe in embracing the past and using the journey to recognize inner strength, beauty, and empowerment. They also recognize this is truly something to be grateful for.

This mother and daughter team have brought together their individual experiences and challenges to promote wellness through gratitude and positivity, no matter the curve balls life throws their way.

Visit their Website at:

Lucylooandroo.com to learn more about Lucy-Loo, Roo, their family, their friends; and of course, the Fairies! And while you're there, be sure to check out their Gratitude Sticks™ so, you can be just like Lucy-Loo and Roo.

Use the Gratitude Stick as a unique and fun way to share good thoughts and experiences with family members. For example, perhaps each night at the dinner table, pass the Gratitude Stick from person to person. Upon receiving the Gratitude Stick, each person says two things they are grateful for and one thing they like about themselves. This can be a very empowering exercise, let alone a surprisingly simple way to talk about one's experiences in a positive and safe environment.

We also suggest performing the same kind of exercise with your children at bedtime. Using the Gratitude Stick in this manner is a wonderful way for your child to fall asleep thinking good thoughts.

Whether it's establishing the Gratitude Stick as a nightly family tradition at dinner or adding it to your child's bedtime routine, you can be sure the exercise is an entertaining way to think about, and to discover, all the good things that we experience every day.

THE GRATITUDE STICK. IT'S EFFECTIVE AND FUN.
PASS IT TO SOMEONE YOU KNOW. YOU'LL SEE!
JUST GRATITUDE IT.

A SPECIAL NOTE
FROM THE AUTHORS

GRATITUDE. An affirmation of goodness. The quality of being thankful. Showing appreciation. Returning kindness.

We like to express gratitude through educational and entertaining stories, and support for our local charities. Visit our website (lucylooandroo.com) and our associated media sites like Facebook and Instagram, to learn more.

What we enjoy most of all is engaging with our audience. We want to hear from you! Let us know how gratitude affects your life (moms, dads, teens, and children). In fact, let us know what kind of ideas you think might make a good story of gratitude that involves Lucy-Loo and Roo! Who knows? Maybe you could be a co-author of one of their adventures! Or at the least, have your thoughts, suggestions and ideas published on our website (lucy-looandroo.com). We look forward to hearing from you! Please email us at info@lucylooandroo.com.

WITH GRATITUDE!

STACEY AND KYRA SCOTT

CPSIA information can be obtained
at www.ICGtesting.com
Printed in the USA
BVHW090632230622
640466BV00003B/8